Just
as well, really!

Written by Jillian Harker
Illustrated by Julie Nicholson

Bright Sparks ☆

Rumpus liked water.

He liked the
drippiness and
dr o pp i ness,

the s p l a s h i n e s s
and sloppiness
of it!

He liked it so much that, whenever there
was water around…

…Rumpus somehow always managed to—

But Mum loved Rumpus, so

every time, she simply sighed—and she mopped up the mess.

Rumpus loved mud.

He loved the way
you could

plodge
in it,

splodge
in it,

slide
in it and
glide
in it!

He loved it so much that, whenever
there was mud around…

...Rumpus somehow always managed to—

But Dad loved Rumpus, so

every time, he simply sighed – and
he sponged off the splatters.

Rumpus enjoyed paint.

He liked to
splatter
and
dash it,

to spread
and
splash
it!

He enjoyed it so much that,
whenever there was paint around…

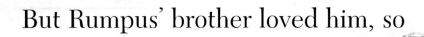
But Rumpus' brother loved him, so

every time, he simply sighed—and he cleaned himself up.

Rumpus liked to find out
how things worked.

He loved the
prodding and
probing,

the **wiggling** and
the
jiggling,
the unscrewing and
the undoing!

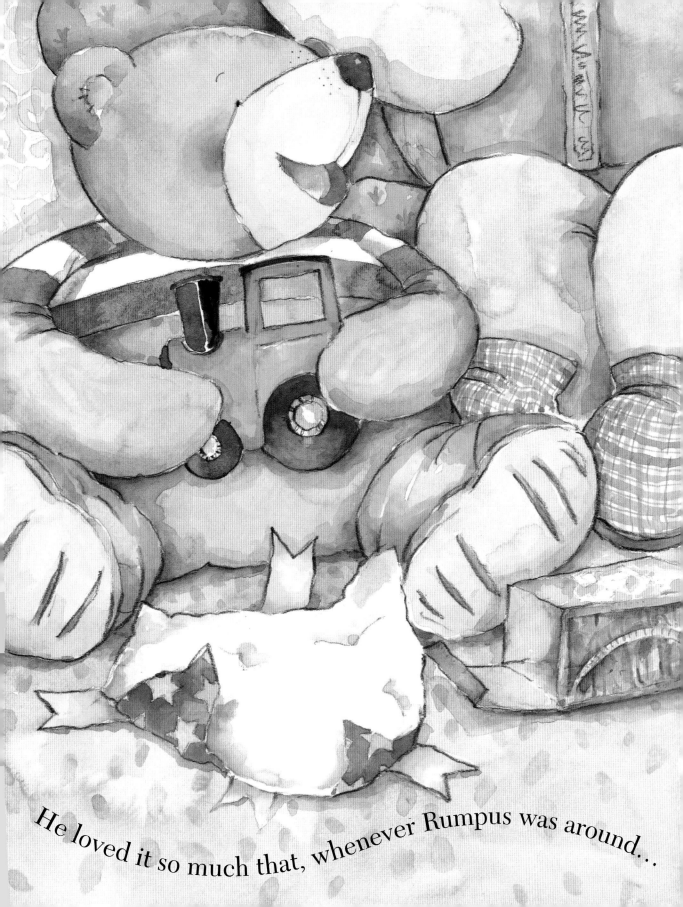

He loved it so much that, whenever Rumpus was around...

...things didn't work for long!

But Granny loved Rumpus, so she simply sighed—and she tidied away the clutter.

Rumpus loved his
mum, dad…

brother and granny…

Rumpus' mum, dad, brother and granny loved Rumpus…

…just as well, really!